A Cheerful Note for Jack

Published by
ROBERTS RINEHART PUBLISHERS
5455 Spine Road
Boulder, Colorado 80301

Published in the UK and Ireland by
ROBERTS RINEHART PUBLISHERS
Trinity House, Charleston Road
Dublin 6, Ireland

Distributed in the U.S. and Canada by Publishers Group West

Printed in Hong Kong

A Cheerful
Note for Jack

WORDS AND PICTURES BY
Arlene Boehm

ROBERTS RINEHART PUBLISHERS

For Meghan Kathleen Rossini

J ack woke up feeling
kind of ho-hum.

Nothing was really wrong...
but nothing was really right.

"Awfully quiet in here,"
thought the bear.

Jack sighed.

Fritz, his cockatiel, was sound asleep, and Jack did not want to wake him.

He decided to go out for a walk.

While Jack was walking along, he noticed something lying on the sidewalk.

It was a funny-looking black squiggle.

What could *that* be for?

Jack found a tiny twig.
He slipped it under the thin,
shiny squiggle and popped
it off the pavement.

Jack pondered
his prize.

"Hmmmm...round at
one end, and pointy
at the other...stiff
but twisty, too!"

He decided to
take it home.

Such a peculiar squiggle!

Jack grew more and more curious. It was sort of like a spoon...

...but it didn't work like a spoon.

Maybe the squiggle
was good for prying
kitchen tins open.

But as Jack wiggled
it under the lid, the
squiggle made a
wobbly little sound...

...and Jack dropped the heavy tin.

It fell to the floor with a thunderous *THWACK!*

Fritz woke up with a startled *SQUAWK!*

But the squiggle bounced lightly from the floor with a delicate *ping!*

"What a lovely sound!" said Jack, as he picked up the squiggle.

Fritz liked it too, and whistled happily at the squiggle...again, and again... and again!

Fritz never acted like *this* before!

Just then, Earl, Jack's neighbor, popped his head through the doorway.

"Oho! Such a joyful noise!" he declared with a smile.

"Earl! Earl! Come and see what I found!" said Jack.

"And what I found too!" announced Earl.

"Oh! Let's show Fritz!" cried Jack.

Fritz was delighted with the squiggles! He shook his bell and whistled new sounds, all while hanging upside-down!

Squiggles and giggles! Jack and Earl
could not stop laughing.

"Whatever can they be?!" exclaimed
the bears.

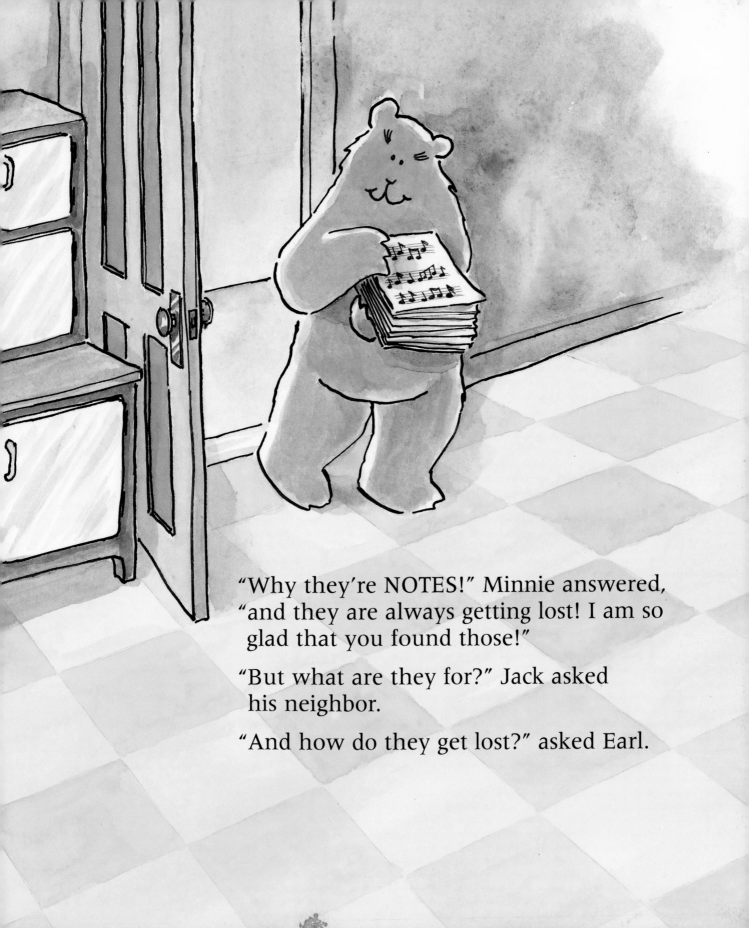

"Why they're NOTES!" Minnie answered, "and they are always getting lost! I am so glad that you found those!"

"But what are they for?" Jack asked his neighbor.

"And how do they get lost?" asked Earl.

"I'll show you." Minnie laughed,
and she began to sing:

*"There are all kinds of notes—
high, low, fast and slow!
Just as letters form a word,
notes make music to be heard!"*

As she sang, the notes began
to dance in the air!

The dancing notes made Jack and Earl feel like dancing too.

*"When you use the notes
to sing, dance and play,
you'll find yourself cheerful,
all through the day...*

*...and now that you're feeling as light as air,
remember that music's for ALL to share"*

ALL indeed!

Like happy butterflies, the sweet notes flitted lightly
through the air, attracting bears from far and near.

"See! There they go again!"
Minnie laughed.

Then Jack had a wonderful
idea and called out from
his window:

"Music's for *ALL* to share!
Quickly, before they float...
every bear catch a note!"

So every bear
caught a note, went
up the stairs and
through the door...

...and together they sang, danced, whistled and snapped,
hummed, stomped, tooted and tapped the day away...

...until bedtime, when the cubs began to yawn.

And as the tired, happy bears said "Good night!" to Jack, he gave each a note to take home.

So now, if *any* bear in Jack's neighborhood wakes up feeling ho-hum, they just take out their note and then...

...well, you
know what
happens!